WARNING

This book contains sexually explicit scenes and adult language. It may be considered offensive to some readers. This book is for sale to adults ONLY.

* * * * * * * * * * * * * * * *

Please store your files wisely where they cannot be accessed by underage readers.

Copyright 2015 by Revelry Publishing

All Rights reserved under International and Pan-American Copyright Conventions. By payment of required fees, you have been granted the non-exclusive, non-transferable right to access and read the text of this book. No part of this text may be reproduced, transmitted, downloaded, decompiled, reverse-engineered or stored in or introduced into any information storage and retrieval system, in any form or by any means, whether electronic or mechanical, now known, hereinafter invented, without express written permission of the publisher.

DISCLAIMER

This book is a work of FICTION. It is not to be confused with reality. Neither the author nor the publisher or its associates assume any responsibility for any loss, injury, death or legal consequences resulting from acting on the contents in this book. The characters, incidents and dialogue are drawn from the author's imagination and are not to be construed as real. While reference might be made to actual historical events or existing locations, the names, characters, places and incidents are either products of the author's imagination or are used fictitiously, and any resemblance to actual persons living or dead, business establishments, events or locales is entirely coincidental. Every character in this book is over 18 years of age. The author's opinions are not to be construed as the opinions of the publisher. The material in this book is for entertainment purposes ONLY. Enjoy.

ISBN-13: 978-1987863451
ISBN-10: 1987863453

Other books by Shyla Starr:

<u>Persuasive Billionaire BWWM Romance Series</u>

Stacey is trying to keep a handle on her life the best that she can. She is on the verge of losing her job and her apartment, while taking care of her sick grandmother. Her life takes an unexpected turn when she meets Charlie, who works for the construction company that is attempting to persuade her to move out of her home.

<u>Tenacious Billionaire BWWM Romance Series</u>

Adalia is too proud to accept help from the billionaire playboy, Trent Dawson. How long can she maintain her resolve? The bank is at her heels to repossess her business. To make matters worse, Adalia finds suspicious evidence of Trent's philandering ways. She must determine whether to trust Trent with the fate of her business and her heart.

<u>Lonely Billionaire Romance Series</u>

Tricia was hired to care for billionaire John's wife, who is dying. An unlikely romance emerges after his wife, Rebecca, gives John permission to pursue his happiness after she is gone.

<u>Ardent Billionaire Romance Series</u>

Deirdre doesn't know what to make of the gorgeous man that seems to be interested in her. His name is Parker Walters and he seems friendly enough. There is just something off about him. Why is he trying the hide the fact that he is the heir to his father's billion dollar software empire?

Fervent Billionaire BWWM Romance Series

Alexandra had never been with a white man before. She had seen William at the café before but she always kept her distance. It was unfortunate that their first chance meeting happened when she dropped her breakfast and spilled coffee all over his expensive business suit.

Audacious Billionaire BWWM Romance Series

Chante is torn between staying close to a man beyond her league, and fleeing from him to spare herself from a hopeless position. But she finds she is propelled into a place where she needs to confront her doubts and cast her fate aside to follow the dictates of her heart. Damned if she does and miserable is she doesn't, how will Chante face the events that will lead her to a place of pure happiness or to the pits of a broken heart?

Get the latest update on new releases from the author at:

https://shylastarr.com/newsletter/

This book is Part Two of the "Elusive Billionaire Romance Series"

1 - Suspicion

Billionaire Hendrick is trying to repair his company's image by putting in some volunteer work, building a school and hospital for the impoverished children in Africa. There, he meets a beautiful African American volunteer, Jocelyn. They hit it off right away but does she belong in his world?

2 - Love Belated

What had Jocelyn done? Why was she being a fool by falling in love so soon? Not trusting her feelings, Jocelyn decided to return home and immerse herself in her work. Perhaps if she kept busy and dated other men, she can forget Hendrick. Things seemed to be going well and a wedding date with her man, Tim, was set. Nothing was going to ruin her day...until a man she was trying to forget shows up the night before the wedding.

3 - Love Amiss

Finally, Jocelyn started her new life with her chosen man. Was it the right decision? At one point or another, she was in love with either Tim or Hendrick. How could that be? The birth of her daughter, Jasmine, was supposed to ground and solidify her marriage. Instead, her partner's jealousy over her past relationship loomed overhead like a dark cloud.

Elusive Billionaire Romance Series

Love Belated

Book Two

By Shyla Starr

Copyright Revelry Publishing 2015

Table of Contents

Chapter One

JOCELYN WAS rushing around like a chicken with her head cut off. To say she was stressed out would be an understatement. She hurried into the cafe around the corner from her studio and grabbed coffee as well as the most delicious donuts for her whole team. She put in her order and tried with all her might to be patient while it was made. She had a huge deadline due that day to provide sketches for a well-known female rock star for an upcoming awards show and she needed everything to go fabulously. She needed this job to bring her career to the next level.

She had been working like a well-trained poodle since she came back from Africa six months prior. She wanted to start making things happen in her life just as she had always imagined. Or maybe it had a lot to do with the man she had left in Africa. She had not spoken to Hendrick since she left and she knew it was the best thing. The man was trouble. It had been a short little fling that she was determined to keep in her past and that was that. She had to question her drive lately and how much that had to do with the fact that she was trying to forget feelings that she had begun to develop with Hendrick. What a fool. What, you fell in love after a few weeks? She wasn't about to believe that and she certainly wasn't going to tie herself pathetically to a man that had never had a serious relationship in his entire life. No thank you.

So she dove into her work with great gusto in the hopes that she could forget the way in which he ignited her body every time he touched her. It had been good for her though; the work she had put into her company in the past six months had grown it significantly. Now she had a team behind her that worked with her in creating her designs. She used to do all the sewing herself and getting everything ready for shows, and now she was able to delegate those tasks to someone else. It was the most empowering and liberating feeling to be in her position. But it also meant she stood in a coffee line stressed to the nines waiting for a beverage. Man, if she could just get this songstress to wear her designs she would be laughing. The girl could virtually wear garbage bags and people went nuts, so having her wear her own designs would definitely benefit her greatly.

Coffee trays in hand she headed for the door. Her team deserved frequent coffee fixes, they had worked so hard, so it was the least she could do for them. Plus in general, she just enjoyed making people happy. When she stepped out into the sun and headed towards her studio she stopped abruptly in the middle of the sidewalk. Screw it, she thought, I'm taking a moment. She stood there on the sidewalk and just pointed her face toward the sky and took a deep relaxing breath. She loved her life and all the great things she had. She was blessed in so many ways and she had no reason to be stressed. With so many people dying in the world, her designs were hardly anything to worry about. And what's more, she was genuinely happy and delighted for her future.

She walked the rest of the way to her office with a new lightness of foot. When she walked into the open concept room, one of her girls ran over and grabbed one of the trays out of her hands.

"Oh thank you. I was so worried I was going to spill coffee and donuts on my way over here."

The girl's name was Samantha and she was Jocelyn's right hand lady. Samantha laughed as she helped Jocelyn with passing out the coffee.

"You got a package today, it looks sort of luxurious."

Jocelyn laughed, "Really? Maybe little miss rock star is trying to bribe my designs in early."

"You don't know who it's from?"

"I couldn't even imagine."

Samantha followed Jocelyn over to her desk and they both stared down at the box. It certainly was an expensively wrapped package and staring at it puzzled Jocelyn further.

"I don't know Jose, it sort of looks romantic."

"Romantic?" Jocelyn laughed and with that she quickly opened the package to find a stunning red dress inside with a necklace that screamed big dollars.

"Oh my god."

"There's a letter, open it!" Samantha practically yelled.

"Okay, okay, I will."

She picked up the letter and turned it over; there was no name or address on it. She opened it and there in simple words was a message to meet at Le Amore, the fanciest restaurant in town. She was to wear the elegant items in the box.

"Who on earth...?"

"It has to be Tim," Samantha squealed.

Jocelyn grew warm all over with the sound of his name. "Really? You think so?"

"Sure he sent you all those flowers last week, of course it's him. He's quite smitten with you."

"I don't know, this is a pretty big jump from flowers."

"Not really, plus he can obviously afford it."

Jocelyn stared hard at the letter willing it to tell her who sent it.

"Should I go?"

"Are you mad? Of course you should go. Some romantic guy sends you this and you're thinking of not going?"

"What if it's Jack the Ripper waiting at the table."

"What are you talking about?"

"Well with all the publicity lately, really this could be anyone."

"You are over-thinking this, you met a great guy last week, it's him for sure. You guys have been talking non-stop since then."

"Maybe you're right."

Samantha left Jocelyn to her own thoughts and returned to her work, coffee in hand. Jocelyn sat down at her desk and read the note again while fingering the beautiful fabric. She knew fabric and this was expensive and she couldn't even guess the amount spent on the necklace. Samantha was right; it was a luxurious package.

Tim came to mind then and she smiled. Would he really have done this? It seemed awful soon for him to be surprising her with such things, but they had hit it off wonderfully so maybe it was him.

She had met Tim just over a week ago at an AIDS benefit. She had been trying to get more involved since she left Africa and she had made a donation of one of her designs to help out. Tim had been seated at her table, on purpose she believed. He was older than her of course and owned one of the major football teams; he was quite successful for a man of his age. Skin the same shade as her own, and a body that was hard all over.

She had been dreaming about that body ever since they met.

They had enjoyed a great night together at the benefit and a friend of hers had mentioned later on in the night that he had requested to sit at her table. She couldn't have been more surprised. They hadn't known each other prior, so what had caused him to want to spend time with her? In the end she had been thankful for his company because she couldn't have imagined the night being better without him. At the end of the night he had asked her to dinner the next night and she accepted without another thought. After a night of lobsters and great conversation, she went home wondering if she had met her match. He was smart, successful and sexy as all hell. And although she dreamed about his body constantly, they had not slept together yet.

Jocelyn smiled again deciding that she was going to go meet her mystery man.

Drinking a glass of wine as she got ready for her dinner date, Jocelyn finally felt relaxed. She got the sketches sent over an hour ahead of schedule and all became well with the world once again. She couldn't wait to get the word on the sketches and wondered how long it would take to get word back on them.

She checked herself in the mirror, the dress fitting like a glove. How had Tim guessed her size so easily without having slept with her? He wouldn't have even had a chance to check out her clothing tags. She gently put the necklace on, feeling its heaviness against her chest. She gasped when she saw the final product of herself. She looked like a movie star. She giggled excitedly, anxious to get to the restaurant to see the look on Tim's face when he saw her in the dress. She left her panties at home, thinking she might give Tim a night he would never forget.

She cabbed it to the restaurant not wanting to have to worry about driving buzzed. She stepped into the gloriously expensive restaurant and waited to be seated. You usually had to wait months to get a reservation there but here she was. Tim must have some serious connections.

She was seated on the terrace to the restaurant, one of the best seats in the restaurant. The view was just breathtaking. She was mesmerized by it when she noticed her date approaching the table.

Her mouth dropped open rather inelegantly and she gaped in surprise as Hendrick approached the table with an ear-to-ear grin. The last time she had seen him was that last morning in Africa. She was startled to find that her heart raced at the sight of him and her temperature rose significantly.

Oh god, what's wrong with me? She was suddenly embarrassed to find her thoughts drifting to a more sexual nature when she saw him smile.

"Well hello Jocelyn, you look absolutely radiant."

"Hendrick, what are you doing here?"

"Should I be alarmed that I'm not the man you were expecting?"

She chose not to answer him and instead just smiled.

"The city may be a big one darling but I can still find you."

"Well this is certainly one way of doing it," she laughed.

He sat down and she instantly felt guilty. She had expected Tim and here sat a man from her past. How would Tim feel if he knew she was here with Hendrick? Her thoughts became torn as she really liked Tim. Liked him so much in fact that she had been having thoughts that included white lace and diamonds. Tim was the perfect guy to marry and start a family with; he would make her incredibly happy. But she had intense chemistry with Hendrick and although she knew there was potential for happiness with Hendrick, she could never truly feel confident that he would be there tomorrow when she needed him.

"So how have you been?" He smiled warmly at her and it lit her up inside.

Jocelyn blushed, "I've been great, I'm actually waiting on a call to see if a celeb is going to use my design."

"Wow, congratulations Jocelyn, though I'm not surprised at all."

She beamed at him from across the table and felt completely at ease with him. They ordered some champagne in celebration of her new potential clients. Dinner just flew by and they talked through the whole dinner unable to stop. It was like they had been without oxygen this whole time and finally found it again. They had talked about her growing business and what he had achieved in Africa. She could tell just by the way he talked that the experience changed him, and for the better. He explained to her what was going on in his case, the fact that it was coming up. He seemed anxious to get it over with and she knew it brought him unnecessary stress.

Just then her phone rang and thinking it was her design team, she told Hendrick she needed to check. She was surprised to see Tim's name flashing on the screen and she immediately sent the call to voicemail. There was no point in trying to talk to him now; that was something she would have to deal with tomorrow. She looked up to see a curious expression on Hendrick's face.

"Who was it?" He had a territorial glint in his eyes that she actually found rather sexy.

"That's none of your business."

Her phone rang again causing her to flush with embarrassment. They both laughed.

"Popular girl tonight."

"I'm sorry."

"No, please, take your time."

She dug her phone out quickly and saw that it was Samantha calling. She answered it promptly and heard the excited chatter of Samantha ringing through the phone.

"Samantha slow down, I can barely understand you."

There was a long pause and Jocelyn's face registered shock.

"Are you serious? Oh wow! I can't believe it, or maybe I can." She started laughing. She quickly said goodbye to Samantha and put her phone away.

"What was that all about?"

Unable to wipe the grin off of her face, Jocelyn took a deep breath trying to calm her heart from racing so much.

"It was my assistant. I got my first celebrity client. My god she just had my sketches for a matter of hours and she already wants me."

Hendrick got up from his chair to go to her. She stood up to accept his hug. "I'm so happy for you Jocelyn." She felt a loss of control when their bodies touched, her mind weakening against the resolve against him. They parted and he looked into her eyes intensely. He kissed her then, right in the middle of Le Amore. She kissed him back.

When they parted he said, "I have a room upstairs, would you like to come up for a bit?"

She nodded unable to speak.

Chapter Two

They entered the penthouse suite without saying a word. As soon as the door closed, Hendrick wrapped his arms around Jocelyn picking her up. He carried her to the master suite, laying her down on the bed.

Her mind was racing as she watched him undress before her. She didn't know if this was the right thing to do and she wondered about her growing feelings for Tim. She was suddenly torn between two men. Her thoughts suddenly shut down when he dropped his underwear. His hard cock stood up, ready for her. She stood up to take off her dress but Hendrick stopped her.

"I want to fuck you with that dress on."

She smiled and crushed his mouth with a kiss searching out his tongue, sucking on it. He moaned and the sound thrilled her. His hands found her bottom and squeezed. She kissed his jawline, nipping at his throat. Her hands found his cock as she played with his balls before bending down. She got down on her knees taking his cock in her mouth.

He let out a long moan his hands lost in her hair. She sucked hard while massaging his balls. His cock hit the back of her throat and he called out her name. She moved in rhythm over his cock, starting off slow then picking up the pace.

"God, Jocelyn that feels incredible."

She continued to suck him twirling her tongue around his tip.

"Darling, I need to be inside you."

She slid him out of her mouth gently as he helped her back up. There was a fire in his eyes and she knew she was in for a night to remember. She lay back down onto the bed, spreading her legs for him. He loved the look of her pussy and he climbed on top of her, lifting her dress to take a look. He was pleased to see no panties and he slid a finger inside. He finger fucked her fast, enjoying the look of ecstasy that came over her face.

"Hendrick come inside me, please. I want you so badly."

Resting her feet on his shoulders he plunged deep inside her. She gasped as the full length of him went inside her, pumping in and out. She called out his name which drove him mad.

"Your pussy feels amazing Jocelyn, I can't get enough of you."

She could barely think as waves of pleasure washed over her continuously. She had lost all ability to think and reason. She only saw him, felt him and she had never felt so complete. She felt a tension build up inside of her and she came on his cock, releasing an orgasm so strong it rocked her body. He came soon after and fell exhausted onto her chest. She kissed his head gently pulling her fingers through his hair. She felt so satisfied she could have fallen asleep right then and there.

Her eyes snapped open. No she was not going to spend the night, absolutely not.

He rolled over and lay on his back, eyes closed breathing deeply. She lay on her side and watched him. He was a handsome man, complicated but handsome.

"Come with me to Greece for a few days."

She laughed loudly. "Umm... no. I have a life here I can't just pick up and go."

"You just got a great client, celebrate, you can take a few days off."

"I have to start work on her dress."

"Start her dress on Monday."

"Hendrick, I can't."

It was their last day in Greece and Jocelyn still couldn't believe she had let Hendrick talk her into going. She had to lie to her staff because she didn't want anyone to know she was taking off with another guy when they knew Tim was around. She had called Tim the next day and explained she would be out of town for a few days, but she would talk to him when

she returned. She needed to make a decision after all;
she couldn't keep carrying on like this.

Hendrick already had the private jet so they left for
Greece immediately, and having never been there it was
everything she had hoped it would be. The first day
however, they hadn't left the room once, the result
being she was sore the entire next day because of it.
They had done very little sightseeing, not that she
cared; it was such a rushed trip that all she wanted to do
was lounge on the beach and soak up some sun.

It had been a great trip so far and she actually
enjoyed the shopping the most. There were some
incredible fabrics there that she snapped up for the
studio. Hendrick spoiled her rotten with clothing and
shoes. Being a billionaire must be something to get
used to.

Now they were lounging by their private pool
sipping margaritas and she couldn't have been happier.
Hendrick left to call in room service so she decided to
check to see if she had any messages. For obvious
reasons she hadn't been checking her messages often
and she noticed two text messages that had come in
from Tim. One was wishing her well on her trip and the
next was a question about how her trip was going. She
sent a quick text back to him asking if he wanted to
grab dinner tomorrow night when she arrived back in
town, because she felt they needed to talk.

She turned around as Hendrick walked back out to
the balcony. He looked annoyed to find her on the

phone. "I ordered in room service so we can relax tonight and catch an early flight in the jet tomorrow."

"Sounds great."

"Is work bugging you?"

She hesitated, "They just want me back, that's all."

He stared at her and she wasn't sure if he believed her. She was surprised when he leaned in to kiss her. He claimed her tongue and roughly squeezed her breasts. She moaned and started rubbing his cock through his shorts. They had taken a day off sex because she had been so sore but she was ready to take him in again.

Their hands were everywhere while their tongues mingled and she felt herself grow wet with yearning. She wanted him inside her immediately.

"Fuck me Hendrick, right now."

She peeled off her bikini top and bottom and ran to the pool and jumped in. She giggled as she reached the surface and he was just plunging in after her. She swam to the shallow end and waited by the edge of the pool. He quickly found her, pushing her up against the wall. His mouth was on hers eagerly and she moaned loudly aching all over her body. She wrapped her legs around his waist and he entered her hard, pumping into her fast. Her body exploded with pleasure and she wrapped her legs around him tighter. He bit into her neck causing her to cry out with pleasure.

"Oh Hendrick, your cock feels so good."

"You're all mine baby."

"Oh it feels so good."

He plunged inside her deep until she came, arching her back into the edge of the pool. He continued to pump inside her harder still until he came.

Exhausted she leaned into his neck and hugged him with her arms. He made her feel incredible; their chemistry just made their sex life so much better.

He pulled apart from her and said, "Let's go see if the food is here." His grin made her laugh and she climbed out of the pool with him. As she towelled herself dry she watched as he went back into the room to check on the room service. She felt so satisfied she could have fallen asleep right then and there.

She quickly checked her phone noticing Tim had messaged her back. She felt guilty once again knowing what she had just done, but in truth she wasn't even dating Tim and they hadn't even slept together. She was just trying to make the best decision possible for herself. His message indicated that he would pick her up at her apartment the next evening. That pleased her so she put her phone away and headed back inside.

Chapter Three

Dinner had been delicious and they lay in the bed talking about the things that were happening for both of them in the next few months. He had ordered up champagne and strawberries and she was enjoying them as they talked. They laughed so easily together she couldn't believe how lucky she was for finding all these great men in her life. She had never had a bad guy in her life and she had no intention of starting with that kind of choice. She just wanted to be happy and fall in love with a great guy. Wasn't that what every girl wanted?

They lay side by side and she thought it was as good a time to talk about the future with him.

"So Hendrick, where do you see this going?"

"What do you mean?"

She sat up laughing, "I mean where do you see this going," she said motioning between the two of them.

"Are we seriously having 'the talk'?"

She was a little put off by his behavior. So in the best firm voice she could muster she said, "Yes Hendrick."

He was silent for a bit and then said, "I thought we were just having fun."

It felt like a weight had dropped in her stomach. "Fun? You're joking right?"

"I don't mean it like that Jocelyn."

"Then how do you mean it?"

He sighed. "I'm not ready for a girlfriend. I have a lot going on right now with the court case and you have things going on too. I enjoy spending time with you but I don't see the need to rush anything right now."

She did not like his answer at all. In fact she hated it. She just stared at him. He could tell that he had upset her. "Look, I'm not saying I don't want something more with you, I just want to take it really slow. I've never been in anything long term and it's a little bit of a shock to the system."

She couldn't at all believe what she was hearing. She felt like slapping him.

"Okay, I think we are on two very different pages here. And had I known that, I wouldn't have flown to Greece with you."

"What are you talking about Jocelyn, what were you expecting, a marriage proposal?"

His words felt like a slap.

"No Hendrick I wasn't looking for a proposal, I was just looking to matter."

She had successfully rendered him silent.

"You can afford another room I'm sure. I would prefer to sleep elsewhere tonight."

"You're not serious."

"Oh but I am."

"You are overreacting."

"Do me a favor Hendrick, don't tell me how I'm feeling. I think things are officially done between us. Please arrange for another room or I will do it myself."

He got up and called to the front desk while she dressed quickly. She gathered together everything she would need for the night.

"I'm sorry Hendrick, I just think we want different things in our lives."

He didn't bother to say anything; she could see he was seething at the thought of her sleeping in another bed.

"I will see you in the lobby in the morning to return home."

It wasn't long before the room service attendant arrived at their room and escorted her to another one. She didn't sleep at all that night.

Once back at her apartment Jocelyn started unpacking. She had a busy night ahead of her and she wanted to be settled before heading out for the night. She was to have dinner with Tim and originally she had planned on letting him down easy. She had believed she was on the road to a future with Hendrick but things hadn't turned out the way she planned. Honestly, who does such a grand gesture as he had just for a little fun? But maybe that's what billionaires did since money was no object after all.

She had been very upset to sleep apart from Hendrick; the whole experience had been upsetting, she couldn't even understand it. The jet ride home had been really long and extremely awkward since neither of them spoke the entire ride home. She could tell he had a lot on his mind, but he never once spoke to her about it. They had landed and he had sent for two separate limos, and that had been the last she had spoken to him.

Her mind was a mess but she wasn't going to cancel on Tim, not after how she had treated him lately. There would be no sex between them however; her mind was too muddled for that.

She quickly got dressed and met Tim down in her lobby.

The next two months flew by and Jocelyn was in a whirlwind of happiness. She couldn't have asked for anything else in life, it was all just pure bliss. After the night that she returned from Greece she had rarely left Tim's side. They had begun a romance that couldn't have gone better for her. She was completely falling so hard for Tim; he was such an incredible man and knowing that he would do anything for her was exactly part of why she loved him so much.

So much had happened over the course of two months: her celebrity clientele had multiplied due to her one client who not only wore her design to the music awards but started to wear her casual styles all over town. She had seen one of her sundresses in a magazine in Europe and she almost died. She and Tim had spent every waking moment together and she just adored him. They had gone on a few day trips to The Hamptons to visit friends of his and she had actually met his parents. She was just... well happy.

She had decided to not tell him anything about Hendrick. It turned out things between them had just been a fling. At no point had he even called to apologize. Just nothing in months. She didn't see any reason to worry Tim unnecessarily. More than that though she didn't want to hurt him for anything. She had been the one foolish enough to believe there had been something between her and Hendrick so there was no need for Tim to get hurt because she was a fool.

She was putting finishing touches on her wardrobe when Tim walked through the door of her apartment. She had considered asking him to move in with her, but after her experience with Hendrick she felt it was too soon.

"My god Jose, you look gorgeous. How on earth did I get so lucky?"

She went to him and kissed him on the mouth. "I'm the lucky one."

"We're both lucky. Are you ready to go my love?"

They headed out the door to go to dinner. He was taking her to an Italian bistro and she couldn't be more excited to eat a ton of pasta. Later they were going to spend the night at his place.

They ordered and chatted casually about the day they each had. She told him about the design she had seen in Europe and he looked at her with pride.

"I wasn't going to do this tonight, I actually wasn't sure when I was going to. Just whenever it felt right I guess."

"What's that baby?"

He pulled out a ring box from Tiffany & Co. and slid it across the table. She stared at it stunned.

"What's in there?"

He laughed, "Well open it and find out silly."

She did just that and gasped when she saw a two-karat princess cut diamond solitaire in a platinum band.

"I fell for you the moment I laid eyes on you, Jocelyn. Please do me the honor of being my wife."

It had been everything that she had wanted. She was dismayed however when Hendrick flashed into her mind at that moment. Shaking her head she wanted to erase him from her mind.

"You're not saying no I hope," Tim laughed nervously.

She looked up at him and smiled. "I'm saying yes."

They hurried to his place after that and as soon as the door closed they started tearing their clothes off. Their mouths joined in lust, intensity and hope for their future. His mouth was on her breasts sucking at her hard nipples and her body arched into his as he did it. She ached between her legs and willed for him to enter her.

"Baby, please, do it now."

"I love when you talk like that."

She was kissing him again and the feeling of his tongue in her mouth made her instantly wet. His hard body was pressed against hers. He lifted her up into his arms and her legs circled his waist. He impaled her on his cock and she moaned loudly.

"Oh Tim, that's so good."

"That's all for you baby."

"Give it to me Tim, oh please. Really good."

He must have had insane upper body strength to keep her in his arms to fuck her properly. He did an amazing job because she was spent and wrapped around his neck while still inside her.

"I love you Jose," he whispered.

"I love you too Tim," she whispered back.

Chapter Four

That night they lay in bed together eating ice cream and watching the late night news. It was something they grew fond of doing together before they turned in for the night. She was surprised to see Hendrick on TV. They were announcing his court case had come to a close and he had been acquitted of all the charges against him. She almost jumped on the bed to celebrate but kept herself composed. She was truly happy for Hendrick, now hopefully he could build up the company in the way he wanted to.

Tim snorted, "Man, what a douchebag that guy is. I wonder how much it cost him to buy himself out of that one."

"What?" Jocelyn was genuinely shocked at what she was hearing.

"Oh ya, that guy is total slime. He knew exactly what was going on there. How could he not?"

"Tim you don't even know him. Those are pretty harsh words for someone you don't even know."

He looked at her strangely. "Babe, why are you getting so defensive? What do you care what my opinion of the guy is?"

Guilt filled her heart and she felt stupid. Why was she arguing with him over a man who treated her like a fling and who she had originally planned on dropping Tim for. She would have lost everything.

"Jocelyn, what is it?"

"I know him, I know Hendrick."

"What? How?"

"I met him on the AIDS mission actually."

"Oh my god. I heard about him going off to save face. Why didn't I connect the two before?"

"There's more. We sort of had a fling for a while. Right up until you and I got really serious actually. I ended things with him."

He sat right up. "Jocelyn, what are you saying to me? How could you get involved with that guy?"

"I'm sorry. I had just met you and you were so great but I was still tangled up with him. I didn't tell you because I didn't want to hurt you."

"So why are you telling me now?"

"I just want things to be perfect between us. I don't want to feel guilt and remorse throughout our marriage. It's out in the open now and I want us to be able to move on from this, because it really is nothing."

She could tell he was very angry with her and he had every right to be.

"I can't believe you did that Jocelyn."

"Baby, please I'm so sorry. I would never purposely hurt you."

She kissed his cheek and took his chin in her hand and forced him to look her in the eyes. "I would never hurt you. Please forgive me."

"You're going to be my wife Jocelyn of course I forgive you. You just bruised my ego a bit."

"There is no need for that. You are the only one that I want." She kissed him again and nuzzled against his chin as he shut off the TV and they went to bed. She knew it wasn't as easy as that. That he would probably lay awake all night thinking about her and Hendrick, but there was nothing she could do about it now. She would just love him as much as she could and make him forget it.

<<◇>>

The wedding is tomorrow, holy crap, she thought. She had been rushing around all day trying to get the last minute details down. She was exhausted. She was looking forward to a peaceful night at home relaxing before she married the man of her dreams in the morning. The bridal party wanted to take her out for dinner and hang out all evening but it wasn't how she wanted to spend her last night. She would be leaving her apartment in a couple of weeks and she just wanted to enjoy it for a moment. She was going to open a bottle of wine and relish her night alone.

Tim had wanted to get married right away; he had
even suggested eloping. Her father however would have
murdered her so the answer was no. She could however
give him a quickie wedding. After meeting with a
wedding planner they had a date set for a month and a
half later. Invites and announcements were sent out
immediately.

The planning went flawlessly and she didn't feel at
all like she had been a Bridezilla. Maybe happiness
does that to a person. Her parents had accepted Tim
with open arms not concerned at all with the speed in
which the wedding happened, which said a lot for Tim's
character.

When she finally arrived at her apartment she was
tired and so looking forward to that bottle of wine. At
least everything was in order as it should be. The
wedding would be wonderfully perfect and they would
be flying out for Paris, France immediately afterwards.
The thought of Paris, the city of love, just tickled her
right around insane. She couldn't wait to experience that
with Tim.

She opened the door to her place, set her bags down
and finally sighed with relief. Everything was finished;
she just had to wait until morning to get married.

She was uncorking the bottle of wine when there
was a knock on the door. Puzzled, she couldn't imagine
who would be showing up now. Everyone knew she
was getting married tomorrow so they would just
assume she didn't want company.

She set the bottle down, and poured a tall glass before going to answer the door. When the door swung open, the glass of wine fell from her hand and smashed on the floor.

"Hendrick, what the hell do you think you are doing here!"

Leaving him at the door stunned, she stomped to the kitchen to retrieve a dustpan and some paper towels. When she returned to the door he was still in the same spot but he offered to clean up the mess for her. She was shaking all over. She was furious that he was there and even more mad at herself when she realized she loved him the moment she saw his face on the other side of the door.

He cleaned everything up and followed her into the living room.

"You better explain to me what you are doing here!"

"I love you."

"Don't you dare say those words to me."

"It's true. I'm sorry, I've been an ass. I tried to fight my feelings for so long and then I saw your wedding announcement and I lost my mind."

"How can you do this to me? It's the night before my wedding."

"I know. I'm disgusting for doing this. I thought I could let you go. But Jocelyn I can't. I need you."

"You should have thought of that months before this," she screamed the words in his face.

"You can't marry this guy."

"Why not? He's going to give me everything you weren't willing to."

"Because you are in love with me too. It's not fair to him."

She threw her hands up in the air. "Like you know anything about being fair."

They stood there staring at each other; Jocelyn's blood pressure was through the roof and he just stood there as calm as can be.

"Hendrick, how could you?" she whispered.

He shrugged. "I am sorry Jocelyn, I wish I would have told you months ago how I felt, but to be honest I thought I had a little more time to figure things out. Like, you don't think you guys might be rushing things a bit here?"

Anger boiled up in her once again. "No, I don't."

"Come on Jocelyn, he's trapping you so you can't find anyone else. That's the only reason why a guy would get married so quick."

"He's not insecure Hendrick, far from it."

"How long have you guys even known each other? Under six months to be sure."

"That doesn't matter. It doesn't change how I feel about him."

His eyes grew angry and she could tell he was holding back some biting comments. The idea of her and another man probably drove him insane.

"How do you feel about me?"

"I want you to leave. My feelings for you don't matter because I am about to marry another man tomorrow."

"I want you to change your mind. Have a future with me instead."

She stared at him and her mind was doing flip-flops while her heart ached for him. There was a part of her, and it would probably always be there, that wanted to run off into the sunset with him. But the truth of the matter was she couldn't trust him. She knew there was a chance she could give up everything for him even now and he would end up flaking out again leaving her alone.

"I tried that already Hendrick. You said you wanted to take things slow. You said you weren't ready."

"So you run off with the first available man that comes around?" he boomed.

"I love him Hendrick. You will not speak that way about him."

"Ya well you love me too, so what are you going to do about that part?"

"Nothing. It will die out eventually."

He snorted, "You and I both know that whatever there is between us will never die out. You can feel it right now can't you? The charge that is between us."

"It doesn't matter. It's too late now."

"Don't do this Jocelyn, please we could be incredible together."

"You're right. We could have been, and I feel like I really tried to have that with you Hendrick. Now I have it with Tim and I'm not going to hurt him for anything."

"You don't belong with a guy like that, you belong with me."

Her heart tore up and her mind began to fog. She didn't know what to do, what to say, or how to get him out of her apartment. God, if Tim decided to surprise her it would be all over with for sure. Maybe that's why Hendrick was there, maybe he was hoping Tim would be there.

"Please leave."

"Jocelyn..."

She looked up into his eyes. "I'm marrying Tim. Now show me some respect and please leave."

He walked away and she followed him to the door. He left silently as she closed the door behind him, locking it. She put her forehead against the door, a tear streaming down her face and whispered, "Goodbye Hendrick."

-To be continued in Book 3-

If you enjoyed this title, I would appreciate your leaving a review of the book. Good reviews encourage an author to write as well as help books to sell. Good reviews can be just a few short sentences describing what you liked about the book without having a spoiler. If you could spend 30 seconds writing a review, I would appreciate it: you can review this title right now at your favorite retailer.

Here is a preview of the **next story** you may enjoy:

Love Amiss - Elusive Billionaire Romance Series, Book 3

JOCELYN AWOKE in the arms of her husband, trying to get rid of the dream that had been plaguing her for weeks. She had now been married for six months to Tim and things weren't going quite as well as she imagined. She started having dreams about Hendrick and she figured it had to do with the fact that her unhappiness level had increased significantly.

It hadn't started out that way; they had returned from their honeymoon and she had moved into his apartment. It was bittersweet leaving her own apartment but she was excited for the future. They began immediately looking for a home to call their own. It wasn't long before they found one they both loved in the country. It was your typical colonial home in all its grandeur. There was a huge guest home in the back of the property that she couldn't wait to use. It allowed peace for themselves as well as their guests. She had a studio as well, but she still managed to drive in every day to her own studio, because she thought better and creation happened as it should.

They had lived in absolute bliss for about a month before things started to change. She wasn't really sure why the change occurred at all. Nothing negative had happened between them; one day things were just different. Tim made her insanely happy and she never regretted for a minute her decision to marry him.

He was attentive and kind and treated her like a queen. She felt safe in his arms and their sex life couldn't have been more fulfilling. He did things to her body and mind that would shock people, but it felt incredible. So, why did he have to go and ruin everything?

She didn't want to be thinking about her past flame, but Tim had changed so much in the past six months she barely recognized him. It was such a short period of time too that she didn't understand why he had proposed at all if things soured for him so quickly and easily. It made her wonder if she had made the right choice after all.

It seemed like they had the perfect marriage for about a month; they spent all their time together, going to events and parties. She often went to football games when he made appearances, which were so much fun to be around because of the noise and energy of the games. They were an amazing team. Then one day he started asking her questions about Hendrick. How long they had been together, why they ended things, how many times they had sex?

She had been shocked at first by his questions and refused to answer them. Her past shouldn't matter she had yelled at him. He was sure that she was still hung up on Hendrick despite the fact that she hadn't spoken to him since the night before their wedding. She asked him to drop it and be happy that they were together and at first he did, but his insecurities crept back in weekly, threatening to destroy them forever.

If you enjoyed this sample then look for **Love Amiss - Elusive Billionaire Romance Series, Book 3**.

Here is a preview of **another book** you may also enjoy:

**Love Astray - Audacious Billionaire BWWM
Romance Series, Book 2**

"**ARE WE** doing spring cleaning?" Markey Green
asked his sister Chante as he eyed the clothes strewn all
over her bedroom floor.

"What? No…no…no…" Chante replied, as she
pulled another hanger from inside her clothes drawer.

"I just need to find the right one…" she added as
she positioned the dress in front of her and stared at her
reflection in the mirror.

She shook her head in disapproval. "Too revealing,"
she muttered under her breathe.

Markey advanced slowly into his sister's bedroom.
He didn't want his wheelchair to run into the dresses
that were piled haphazardly on the floor.

"Must be a hot date then," he smiled with
amusement as his sister began to attack the shelves
where her shoes rested.

Chante stopped momentarily. She was surprised at
her brother's spontaneous perception. She smiled trying
to mask the concern in her eyes. He had grown so much
thinner these last few months. His ALS had progressed
so much faster than she thought.

"And what do you know about having a hot date,
hmmm…" she said as she tousled his hair.

"Well…enough to notice that you're excited once again. These last few months you just seemed… sad." Markey replied.

Chante felt a twinge of guilt. She honestly didn't realize her brother noticed at all.

"Was I that bad…" she asked as she sat down on the bed.

"Bad? Nah, you were just sad." Markey answered wryly.

"Yeah, I guess I was…but I'm ok now…so don't you worry about me kid." Chante replied.

She never told him about the way she felt. In fact she hasn't told anyone about it. Who would believe her anyway? It isn't everyday that a good-looking and wealthy... very wealthy... Jared Lowell asked you to be his sex toy.

Chante tried to forget everything that happened that day on the roof deck of NY General Hospital. She remembered him calling her name as she pushed the metal doors aside and ran towards the freight elevator. She punched the button on the lift and went all the way to the basement where she knew she would be safe. She was confused, her mind was in a whirl, and she wanted to stay away from prying eyes. She stopped by a wall and there amidst rows of empty cars she slumped down on the hard cement floor as despair and disillusionment brought waves of tears that shook her to the core.

"How dare him…" she muttered disconsolately, "he must think I'm scum."

Jared Lowell, heir to the fortunes of Lowell Enterprises had just offered to keep her as a mistress in exchange for a condo and for "stuff" as he called it, even having the impudence to conclude "that's what girls like…"

But Chante didn't have the heart to put all the censure on the scoundrel. She was partly to blame too, remembering what happened between them in the bathroom of the suite where his mother was a patient.

"Shit…" she whispered between her tears.

But it was too late now for regrets. It happened and she had to live with it. In hindsight, she was confused why she even allowed it to come about. Had the patient, Samantha Lowell, or Nurse Betty, and Director Whittle come back and caught them in the illicit act, she would have lost her job as Certified Nursing Assistant, that's for sure.

It was with uncertainty that she reported for work the very next day. She had vowed the night before that she would refuse adamantly, beg even, not to be assigned to Suite 247 once again. But the floor seemed unusually quiet that morning. She learned that Samantha Lowell was discharged the night before. The private helicopter that brought her in brought her out, as well.

"Oh, thank God," was Chante's initial reaction.

She didn't have to suffer the awkwardness of seeing Jared again. Admittedly, she liked Mrs. Lowell. She felt a certain degree of kinship with the older woman. It made her a little sad, thinking she didn't get a chance to say goodbye.

But as the initial relief swept through her body, she was also assailed with a deep sense of melancholy. She won't be seeing Jared Lowell anymore. That, at least, was its own blessing, Chante thought.

The weeks that followed their departure, Chante often had to struggle with her feelings. She tried to focus on her work but often found herself looking out into space. She felt miserable, disconnected, and it took all her effort to keep going about her duty. The world lay heavily on her shoulders.

Nurse Betty took her aside and asked what was bothering her. Chante couldn't look her in the eye. The woman was very perceptive.

"Is this about a man?" Nurse Betty inquired.

Chante nodded her head. The supervisor didn't have to know who. So Chante decided on a half-lie.

"Yes…but it's over now…" Chante answered.

"That's good. If it didn't last too long, then he must be the wrong guy for you. Get out of that hole you crawled into. Someone better should come along for you." The supervisor consoled her.

Chante nodded her head in agreement. Nurse Betty didn't know how close to the truth she was. Jared

Lowell was definitely the wrong guy for her. It's about time she moved on and forgot all about him.

Things were slowly getting back to normal.

If you enjoyed this sample then look for **Love Astray - Audacious Billionaire BWWM Romance Series, Book 2**.

Here is a preview of **another story** you may enjoy:

Love Divested: Persuasive Billionaire BWWM Romance Series, Book 2

DOWNSTAIRS IN the lobby, Stacey saw a woman who was, clearly, not a tenant. The stranger looked like she belonged in a fashion magazine.

Trying to be helpful, Stacey asked, "Hi, are you lost?"

The woman looked Stacey up and down before answering. "Yes, I believe so. I'm looking for someone."

"Who are you looking for?"

"Charlie Albert. He had business here before he mucked up the deal. Have you seen him?"

Stacey's heart raced. "Uh, no. No, not for a few days. Who are you?" It was a bit blunt, but she couldn't help herself. Who was this woman?

The woman lowered her glasses and replied, "I'm Charlie Albert's fiancée, not that it's any business of yours."

Stacey thought she misheard the woman. There had to be some sort of mistake. There was no way that this woman was Charlie's fiancée.

"I'm Adele," the woman went on, oblivious to Stacey's inner turmoil. "I wanted to surprise him, you see. I've been overseas. His assistant said he had been here a couple times, so I thought he could be here now."

"Sorry, he hasn't been here since the apartments were dropped from the rebuilding plan." Stacey hoped her voice sounded as if she had no interest in Adele or her claims of being Charlie's fiancée.

Adele wrinkled her nose. "That's a shame. I suppose I'll try him elsewhere then. Now that I'm here, though, I can understand why he would leave as quickly as possible." She laughed.

Stacey wanted to tell this strange, uppity woman that this was her home. She didn't need strangers coming around running their mouths off about how little they thought of it. But she couldn't bring herself to say anything. Instead, she could only stare at Adele, who was looking around the lobby one last time.

"Well, thank you for the help, dear," Adele said and left the apartment complex in her towering high heels without a backward glance.

Stacey just stood there. Her head was spinning as if everything had suddenly been uprooted. Part of her wanted to chase after Adele and ask her just how she could be Charlie's fiancée.

But a sick, swooping feeling was slowly consuming Stacey. She had to talk to Charlie as soon as possible. She fumbled for her phone and brought up his number. The phone rang three times before a man answered.

"Charlie Albert's phone." The man's voice was deep and somehow familiar although it wasn't Charlie.

No one had ever picked up Charlie's cell phone before and it threw Stacey off guard. She stumbled over her words. "Hi, uh, hello. This is Stacey, and, um, I'm Charlie's—" What was she, exactly? His girlfriend? Or just a girl on the side?

"Stacey!" the man exclaimed as if he knew her. "This is Tony."

In her haze, it took her a few seconds to remember who Tony was. The image of him smiling at her on board his yacht floated back to Stacey.

"Right, hi Tony!" She feigned a cheerfulness. "How are you? Your yacht was very lovely."

"Glad you enjoyed it. I enjoyed seeing you on it."

The remark startled her. His tone had been warm and almost flirtatious. That's odd, she thought to herself.

"I'm calling for Charlie," she blurted out and cringed.

She probably sounded incredibly rude. She was blowing off what Tony had just said. But Stacey had no idea what to make of it and couldn't focus on that right now. The image of smug Adele still danced in her memory.

"He's in a meeting. He's running late, actually, because we had a meeting of our own. That's how I have his phone," Tony joked, "but I can pass him a message."

"Yeah, please. Let him know I called and would appreciate a call back."

"Of course. I had no idea you two were so, well, close," Tony replied tactfully.

For one wild second, Stacey wanted to ask Tony about Adele. He would know, wouldn't he? Tony and Charlie seemed to be friends and ran in the same social circles. But she stopped herself before she could do something so silly. No, whatever was going on was something she would ask Charlie directly. She would not go behind his back.

"Thank you! I have to go to work now. Have a nice day!" Her voice was too high-pitched as she tried to hide her emotions. It just made her sound crazy and somewhat desperate.

She ended the call and headed to work, telling herself that she would get to the bottom of it soon enough.

Although Stacey had promised herself not to dwell on Charlie and Adele, it proved to be impossible. The restaurant had one lone customer—an old lady sitting at a booth asking for coffee non-stop as she read a book.

Maria bustled into the kitchen about two hours into her shift and looked over at Stacey. "I quit."

"What? That just leaves me and Amanda."

Maria shrugged. "Not my problem. I'm going to go fucking mental if I stay here a second longer. See you around."

Stacey stared as Maria headed toward the break room. She hadn't ever been exactly close with Maria so she hadn't been expecting a tearful goodbye. But a mumbled 'see you around' was a pretty shitty farewell.

Tears formed in Stacey's eyes. She turned away to face the wall. *What is wrong with me?* She tried to regroup. Normally, someone quitting wouldn't affect her like this.

She left the kitchen, leaving Brad behind playing a game on his phone and found William in his office. She knocked on the door, and he looked up at her.

"You're not quitting too, are you? I was hoping to run with a skeleton crew until we closed, but it's turning more into a ghost crew at this point."

"Nope, I'm here 'til we close," Stacey replied. "I have a job lined up afterward already."

"Amanda mentioned that the other day. Congrats."

Working at another diner didn't seem like something to be congratulated about. Out of the blue, her sister's words from their last fight haunted her. *All you do is work at some dead-end job without ever trying to better yourself or move onto something new.*

If you enjoyed this sample then look for **Love Divested: Persuasive Billionaire BWWM Romance Series, Book 2**.

Other Books by Shyla Starr

- Persuasive Billionaire BWWM Romance Series

- Tenacious Billionaire BWWM Romance Series

- Lonely Billionaire Romance Series

- Ardent Billionaire Romance Series

- Fervent Billionaire BWWM Romance Series

- Audacious Billionaire BWWM Romance Series

Get the latest update on new releases from the author at:

https://shylastarr.com/newsletter/

About the Author - Shyla Starr

Shyla currently specializes in writing interracial romance stories and is a huge fan of the alpha male. Simply put, there just aren't enough stories about mixed couple romances, which is something she is aiming to fix.

Being a bookworm all her life, when Shyla discovered men she also realized how easy it was to fulfill her fantasies through her writing.

When not writing and fantasizing about men, Shyla enjoys dancing, reading and chilling with her friends.

Connect with Shyla Starr

I really appreciate you reading my book! Here are my social media coordinates:

Friend me on Facebook:
https://www.facebook.com/shylastarrauthor

Follow me on Twitter: https://twitter.com/shylstarr

Check me out on Goodreads:
https://www.goodreads.com/author/show/8436084.Shyla_Starr

Subscribe to my newsletter:
https://shylastarr.com/newsletter/

Visit my website: https://shylastarr.com/

www.ingramcontent.com/pod-product-compliance
Lightning Source LLC
Chambersburg PA
CBHW031631200726
48288CB00019B/1373